# HERE NOW BREATHE

A Weightlessness Story by **Tom Fazio**

Illustrated by **Zhu Haibo**

*For the Children. Be Weightless.*

"What's wrong Cayden? Why are you sad?"

"I'm an unlucky guy," said Cayden. "I had a bad day at school. I don't want to go back. I...I don't know if I can do it like the others."

"Oh buddy," said Cayden's mother. "Let me tell you a story about a girl who also had a bad day at school."

"A long time ago a girl traveled with her father to a school far away..."

"Where are we? Why are we here dad?" Chrissy asked.

Her father replied, "This is a special place. There's only one reason people come here sweetie, and that's to learn to breathe."

"Learn to breathe?" she pondered.

"But I already know how to do that."

5

"Chrissy, this is Master Shi," said her father. "He's going to look after you for a few days. Listen carefully to him and do everything he tells you."

"You're leaving me here...alone?" she asked with concern.

"It must be alone," said her father. "But you'll be just fine. I promise!"

"Ok," said Chrissy.

"We need to fetch water before we can eat breakfast," explained one of the students.

"That's a lot of stairs," thought Chrissy.

"What's wrong Chrissy?" asked Master Shi.

"It's just...I can't do it. I'm not strong enough," she replied.

"Not strong enough for what?" asked Master Shi.

"I'm not as strong as the others. I can't make it to the top. My arms hurt and my legs hurt. I'm so tired," said Chrissy.

"I see," replied Master Shi.

Chrissy realized she's very far from the top.

"The water is so heavy," thought Chrissy. "And I'm still so so far away. How can I do this?"

"Chrissy, what do you hear right now? And what do you feel?" asked Master Shi.

"Right now?" she said. "I hear nothing. I feel tired. I'm afraid I can't make it."

"Let's rest for a moment. Tell me," asked the master, "Do you hear your breath?"

"Yes," she noticed.

"Listen to it very carefully for a few moments. Feel it flow all the way down to fill up your belly. And tell me what else you hear."

"I...I hear birds," she said. "I hear the students laughing and talking at the top of the hill."

"And right now, while you listen, do you still feel tired? Do you still feel pain?" he asked.

"Right now? No. I guess I don't feel pain right now," replied Chrissy.

"Then why are you afraid?" questioned the master. "You feel no pain. There is nobody watching you. It's just you and me."

14

Listening carefully, she realized that at that moment there was nothing wrong. There was no pain. There was nothing to fear. But then she looked up and remembered, "But it's still so far."

"Ah yes, the stairs," said the master. "Let me ask, can you take just one more step Chrissy?"

"Yes, I guess I can take one more," she admitted, "But..."

"Let's do that," said the master. "Just one more. Look only at that next step, and observe your breath."

After she took a step Master Shi asked if she could take one more step. And she did. And another. And another, watching her breath the entire time.

"Chrissy," said the master, "It's time to look up."

"I...I made it!" Chrissy said with surprise.

"You made it," said Master Shi. "One step at a time. It's time for breakfast."

The students cheered for her.

The children giggled as Chrissy fumbled around with her chopsticks.

"Eating noodles and dumplings with sticks? This is a funny place," she thought. "Are you sure these sticks are for eating?" she asked.

"After breakfast I'll show you something special," said Master Shi. "Try to figure those things out."

"Chrissy, these are the Masters of Lightness," explained Master Shi. "Very few people will ever know about them. They have been dedicated to this life since they were your age. They resemble what all of us can become with very hard work."

"Wow, how do they do that?" Chrissy couldn't believe people could be so capable.

"I'll tell you something more Chrissy," continued the master. "Do you see that man with the chains? Would you believe me if I told you that on his first day, he too could not climb the stairs?"

"That's impossible," blurted Chrissy. "He's the strongest person in the world! How can that be?"

"He learned to breathe," said the master, "Just like you. He saw that his fear was only about things that did not happen yet. And he saw that all his pain was only in the past. But right now, in this moment, listening to his breath, there is no pain. And there is no fear. And just like you he took one more step. And then another. And when the stairs became easy for him he added weights to his ankles. And when that became easy he added chains around his neck."

"Why would he do that?" she asked.

"Because when he removes the weight that holds him down he feels very light. He feels weightless," the master explained.

"What is this?" Chrissy asked.

"This is to remind you to breathe," said Master Shi, as he handed her a pendant. "A fallen leaf is in-between life and death. It is precious,and it's here for only a few short moments. This is to remind you to be where you are and to listen to your breath. It's to remind you that with only one full breath you too can be weightless."

"Were you a good girl Chrissy? What did you learn while I was away?" asked Chrissy's father.

"I learned how to be strong," replied Chrissy.
"I learned how to breathe!"

"Can you teach me to breathe Mom?" asked Cayden.

"Of course," said Cayden's mother. "There are not many rules, but when you breathe it's helpful to sit straight and to relax your shoulders. Then simply watch your breath. Feel it flow in and out naturally from your belly, not your chest. You must be still, and listen very carefully.

Feel what you feel.

After a few moments she asked Cayden how he feels.
"I feel weightless, Mom," said Cayden.

"It's time I give this to you. It's to remind you to breathe, no matter where you are and no matter how you feel."

"Where did you get this?" Cayden asked puzzled.

"My teacher gave it to me," replied Chrissy.

Be Weightless

**For the adults:**

If you like the message in this book and would like to learn more about Weightlessness (the grown-up version!) for yourself, you can join my free newsletter and visit:

**www.weightlessness.co/#join-the-tribe**

As a self-published author I rely largely on word of mouth to share Weightlessness. If you feel this book can help more youngsters face their challenges with greater courage please consider leaving an Amazon.com review or recommending the book to a friend.

I'd be grateful. Thank you.

Made in the USA
Columbia, SC
29 March 2019